CLASSROOM CRITTERS

PARTY TIME

by Molly Beth Griffin

illustrated by Colin Jack

CONTENTS

CLASSROOM CRITTERS

**These five friends live within the walls,
nooks and crannies of a primary school.
They learn alongside the children every day,
even though the children don't see them!**

STELLA

Stella is a mouse. She loves her friends. She also loves children and school! She came into the school on a cold winter's day. She knew it would be her home forever. Her favourite subjects are history and music. She is always eager for a new day to start.

BO

Bo is a parakeet. He is a classroom pet. The friends let him out of his cage so they can play together. Bo loves to read. He goes home with his teacher at the weekend, but he always comes back to school to see his friends.

DELILAH

Delilah is a spider. She has always lived in the corners of the school. She is so small the children never notice her, but she is very clever. Delilah loves maths and computers and hates the broom!

NICO

Nico is a toad. He used to be a classroom pet. A child forgot to put him back into his tank one day. Now he lives with his friends. The whole school is his home! He can be grumpy, but he loves science and art. As Nico doesn't have fingers, he paints with his toes!

GOLDIE

Goldie is a goldfish. She is very wise. The friends ask her questions when they have a big decision to make. She gives good advice and lives in the library.

A SPECIAL WEEK

Chapter 1

It was the last week of school, and Stella the Mouse couldn't believe her luck!

"It's just one fun thing after another!" she told her friends. "And I love parties!"

On Monday, there was a music concert. Hidden under the benches, Stella sang her heart out. Her friends cheered.

On Tuesday, Nico the Toad hung his best painting in the corridor art show.

The friends looked at all the children's beautiful drawings, paintings and sculptures.

"Amazing!" Nico said.

On Wednesday, Delilah the Spider watched over the maths competition.

She answered almost every question correctly, even if no one heard her.

On Thursday, Bo the Parakeet joined in the spelling contest. He misspelt the word *ankylosaurus*.

"It's even one of my favourite dinosaurs!" he said. His friends hugged him tight.

On Friday, the friends watched the children play outside at the school picnic.

Stella didn't think life could get any better.

Chapter 2

THE GOODBYE

But then, something horrible happened. When the picnic was finished and the children headed for the school buses to go home, the teachers went too. Every single one of them.

The teachers stood on the pavement. They waved to the children as the buses drove away.

The children waved back.

"Goodbye, goodbye!" they called.

"Have a good summer!" the teachers called.

"Oh no!" said Stella. "The children are going away? Forever?"

"Summer?!" said the friends.

The teachers walked back inside the school. Stella sniffed. She thought her heart would break.

"What about me?" said Bo. "Will I have to go home with the teacher for the summer?"

Stella gasped. "Let's go and ask Goldie."

The friends rushed to the library.

They could always ask Goldie when they had a problem. She knew what to do.

"Goldie, it's summer. The children have gone. Will Bo have to go away all summer too?" Stella asked.

Goldie swam in a circle.

"Blub, blub," she said. That meant no. At least they thought it did.

"No?" said Bo. "I can stay here? Or at least, I can come and visit?"

"Blub," said Goldie. That meant yes.

"Yay!" said Stella. "But Goldie,

will the school be empty all summer?"

"Blub, blub," said Goldie.

"Oh, good!" Stella said.

She was relieved, but she had no
idea what summer would bring.

Stella missed the children already. She wanted her happy routines to go on forever.

She loved learning alongside the children every day. She loved helping the teachers.

What would she do every day now? Why did things have to change at all?

NEW KINDS OF FUN

The next morning, loud music woke up Stella and her friends. Stella followed the music, her friends right behind her.

The teachers were back and had turned on the radio. They were cleaning out their classrooms.

"Watch out!" said Delilah.

The broom rushed past. It was moving really fast. Then the mops zoomed by!

The caretakers had to deep clean the school while the children were away.

The clearing out and cleaning up went on for days. The friends helped when they could.

They stayed out of the way when brooms and mops came past. At one time a huge machine whirred past to wax the floors. Yikes!

Soon the teachers were gone too. The friends didn't know what to do. But the school quickly filled with people again.

The building buzzed with summer classes and camps. There were so many fun things to try.

Stella discovered
the marching band.

Nico tried out a pottery class.

Delilah learnt
how to skip.

Bo's teacher taught summer school classes, so he was at school a lot. Bo went to book clubs. And story times. And writing club!

The friends had fun trying new things. They'd been so worried about the summer. Now they didn't want the summer to end!

Before long the teachers came back. They planned their lessons. They organised and decorated their rooms. The animal friends secretly helped out.

Nico made the noticeboards pretty. Delilah sorted the pencils. Bo put the books in order.

Stella scurried around, helping everyone. She wanted everything to be perfect for the children when they returned.

Summer had been more fun than the friends had expected. But nothing was more fun than a new school year!

TALK ABOUT IT

1. The last week of school often includes fun activities. What is your favourite activity at the end of the school year?

2. Which one of the Classroom Critters are you most like? Why?

3. The animals always ask Goldie for advice. Who do you go to for advice? Why?

WRITE ABOUT IT

1. Write about a summer club that you would enjoy going to.

2. Make a list comparing how you felt on the first day of school and on the last day.

3. Write a short story about what you think teachers do during the summer.

MOLLY BETH GRIFFIN

Molly Beth Griffin is a writing teacher at the Loft Literary Center in Minneapolis, Minnesota, USA. She has written numerous picture books (including *Loon Baby* and *Rhoda's Rock Hunt*) and a YA novel (*Silhouette of a Sparrow*). Molly loves reading and hiking in all kinds of weather. She lives in South Minneapolis with her partner and two children.

COLIN JACK

Colin Jack has illustrated several books for children, including *Little Miss Muffet* (Flip-Side Rhymes), *Jack and Jill* (Flip-Side Rhymes), *Dragons from Mars*, *7 Days of Awesome* and *If You Happen to Have a Dinosaur*. He also works as a story artist and character designer at DreamWorks Studios. Colin splits his time living in California, USA, and Canada with his wife and two children.

Raintree is an imprint of Capstone Global Library Limited, a company
incorporated in England and Wales having its registered office at 264
Banbury Road, Oxford, OX2 7DY – Registered company number: 6695582

www.raintree.co.uk
myorders@raintree.co.uk

Illustrated by Colin Jack
Designed by Ted Williams

Shutterstock: AVA Bitter, design element throughout,
Oleksandr Rybitskiy, design element throughout

Original illustrations © Capstone Global Library Limited 2020
Originated by Capstone Global Library Ltd
Printed and bound in India

ISBN 978 1 4747 7179 5

British Library Cataloguing in Publication Data:
A full catalogue record for this book is available from the British Library.